GREG the SAUSAGE ROLL

SANTA'S LITTLE HELPER

To Phoenix and Kobe,
never give up on your dreams.
Love Mum and Dad xx – R. H. and M. H.

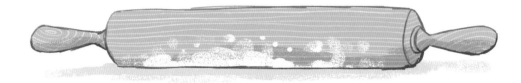

For James,
finally immortalized in print alongside Christmassy baked goods.
It's what he would have wanted x – G. C.

PUFFIN BOOKS

UK | USA | Canada | Ireland | Australia | India | New Zealand | South Africa

Puffin Books is part of the Penguin Random House group of companies whose addresses can be found at global.penguinrandomhouse.com.

www.penguin.co.uk   www.puffin.co.uk   www.ladybird.co.uk

Penguin
Random House
UK

First published 2021

001

Text and illustrations copyright © Mark and Roxanne Hoyle, 2021

The moral right of the authors has been asserted

Printed and bound in Italy by L.E.G.O. S.p.A.

The authorized representative in the EEA is Penguin Random House Ireland, Morrison Chambers, 32 Nassau Street, Dublin D02 YH68

A CIP catalogue record for this book is available from the British Library

ISBN: 978-0-241-54833-2

All correspondence to:
Puffin Books, Penguin Random House Children's, One Embassy Gardens, 8 Viaduct Gardens, London SW11 7BW

GREG the SAUSAGE ROLL

SANTA'S LITTLE HELPER

MARK AND ROXANNE HOYLE

Illustrated by Gareth Conway

PUFFIN

IT WAS CHRISTMAS EVE in the bakery.
Greg the sausage roll was swinging merrily on high
from the sparkly bright red tinsel.

Wheeeee!

"Chill out, Greg!" said Frosty the meringue snowman.
"Chill out?" cried Greg mid-swing.
"But it's CHRISTMAS, the most wonderful time of the year!
I wish I had a Christmas jumper!"

Greg leapt on to the pastry counter and landed next to his sausage-roll sweetheart, Gloria, just as the bakery door jingle-jangled open.
"Sorry!" called the baker.

I'm closing!

"But we need a mince pie!" wailed the boy.
"I think we're too late," said Mum. "Better try somewhere else."
Then something – or rather, *someone* – caught the boy's eye.
"What about a sausage roll for Santa?" he said.

"A sausage roll?" said Dad. "Great idea! We'll have that one, please."

And he pointed to . . .

GREG!

"Merry Christmas, Gloria!" Greg whispered as he was popped into a paper bag.

"Jingle bells, jingle bells, jingle **alllll** the way!"
sang Greg from inside his bag.

"Ooh," he wondered.
"Which way *are* we going?"
He peeked out . . .

WOOF!
WOOF! WOOF!

"Stop it, Rocky!" grumbled a lad.
"Woof to you too, pup!" called Greg.

He turned to look at
his new home.

WOW!

Then Greg was plucked out of the buggy, whizzed through the front door and marched straight into the living room where he went

up!

Up!

Up on to the mantlepiece.

"There you are – all ready for Santa,"
said the boy, beaming.
Greg was SO excited.

As night fell,
the house grew quiet.

Then suddenly . . .

"OI, OI!" boomed a voice into the silence.
Greg nearly jumped out of his pastry.

"What 'ave we 'ere then?" said the voice.
It was an elf beside Greg on the shelf.

Before Greg could reply, the carrot jumped to his feet!
"EXCUUUUUUSE ME!" he cried. "You're not a mince pie! What about tradition?"

"Never mind that," the elf interrupted.
"New boy, it's your job to treat Santa to . . .
A CHRISTMAS TREE WRAPPED IN TOILET PAPER!"

Greg leapt up from his plate.
"Can I get the toilet paper now? Can I? Can I?"
"YES, MATE!" cheered the elf.

"*Please* be good –" came an angelic voice from somewhere up high.

"Oh, come on," interrupted the elf again.
"How about a BAUBLE FIGHT?"

"For goodness' sake!"
cried the angel,
and with that she fainted.

But before Greg and the elf could make any mischief,
they heard something on the roof. Could it be ... FOOTSTEPS?

It wasn't just any footsteps – it was SANTA!
Greg's tummy rolled with excitement.

SPECIAL DELIVERY

THUD

Santa stood up tall and *his* tummy rumbled with hunger!
"HO, HO, HO!" he chuckled, peering at Greg.
"This will do very nicely. I'm full to the beard of mince pies!"

Santa reached out his arm . . .
But he was startled by a loud CREEEEEEEEEEEAK!
Was someone AWAKE upstairs?!

Quick as a flash, Santa stashed the presents under the tree,
stuffed Greg in one pocket, Mr Carrot in the other –
and scrambled back up the chimney!

As Greg slid down into Santa's pocket,
he had a lovely soft landing.
"Hello, it's SUCH a pleasure to meet you!"
exclaimed the Nice List.

"Get off me!"
grunted the
Naughty List.

Greg was trying to decide what to say when a big hand appeared . . .

"I'm about ready for a snack," said Santa.

"Hello! I'm Greg!" giggled the excitable little sausage roll.
"Can't believe I'm finally meeting you, Santa.
Can I help you deliver all the presents? Can I? Can I pleeeeeease?"

"Come on then," said Santa.
"My snack can wait. But it's cold up
here, so let me see what I've got . . ."

Santa gave Greg a tiny parcel and inside . . . at last . . .
"A CHRISTMAS JUMPER!" he squealed.

Santa smiled, picked up the reins and

WHOOOOOOOSH!

They were off.

At the first house, Greg had to be QUICK!

Run!
Run!
Run!

Who's a pretty sausage roll then?

At the second house, Greg had to tread *very* carefully.

ROLL! ROLL! ROLL!

At the third house, Greg had to be *oh so* quiet.

Shhh! Shhh! Shhh!

At the fourth house, Greg had to NOT look down!

Stretch! Stretch! Streeeeetch!

"What a team!" cheered Santa as the sleigh continued to WHOOSH through the sky. "Dasher and Dancer and Prancer and Vixen – we've almost finished!"

Greg punched the air.
"Go, reindeers!" he cried.

SPECIAL DELIVERY

Suddenly the sleigh started to wobble and the smallest reindeer burst into tears. "I'm so tired!" she sobbed.

And, before they knew it, the sleigh was hurtling towards the nearest rooftop . . .

... where it landed with a ginormous

CRASH!

Greg flew out of his seat, flipping over and over in the air until . . .

TWANG!

He found himself DANGLING in front of the hungry reindeers!

"Hi there!" said Greg.

The reindeers couldn't resist those wafts of puff pastry. They found a new burst of energy and the sleigh climbed higher and higher.

"That's more like it!" cried Santa.

Nostrils flaring, the reindeers lunged upwards, drooling until . . .

OOPS! The thread of Greg's jumper finally went snap!
"MERRY CHRISTMAS, GREG!" Santa called.
"MERRY CHRISTMAS, SANTA! I love yoooouuuuuuuu!"

Greg drifted . . .

down,

down,

Twit-twoo!

down

into a red-brick chimney.

"Ow!
   Ow!
      OW!"
exclaimed Greg as sharp prickles spiked his bottom.

At last he rolled over on to a soft fluffy rug.

As Greg gazed up, he spotted the most beautiful sight in the world.

"GLORIA!" Greg cried.
"I met Santa!
And he LOVES sausage rolls!"

"Welcome home, Greg!"
said Gloria, smiling.

IT'S
CHRIIIISTMAAAAS –
let the good times roll!